Chess Rumble

by **G. NERI**

art by **JESSE JOSHUA WATSON**

Lee & Low Books Inc. New York

To my family, who is eternally patient and supportive.
To my writing groups, who consistently make me better.
To Karen Bachman and her middle school readers, who gave me confidence.
To my editor, Jennifer Fox, who guided me through the jungle.
And to Chess Mentors like Eugene Brown, who help turn
young pawns into kings—G.N.

For my Queen, Mariah Evergreen—J.J.W.

Text copyright © 2007 by G. Neri
Illustrations copyright © 2007 by Jesse Joshua Watson

LEE & LOW BOOKS Inc., 95 Madison Avenue, New York, NY 10016
leeandlow.com

Manufactured in China

Book design by Cohava (Cookie) Dodo
Book production by The Kids at Our House

The text is set in Univers Condensed
The illustrations are rendered in acrylic

10 9 8 7 6 5 4 3 2 1
First Edition

Library of Congress Cataloging-in-Publication Data
Neri, Greg.
Chess rumble / by G. Neri ; art by Jesse Joshua Watson. — 1st ed.
p. cm.
Summary: Branded a troublemaker due to his anger over everything from being bullied to his sister's death a year
before, Marcus begins to control himself and cope with his problems at home and at his inner-city school when an
unlikely mentor teaches him to play chess.
ISBN 978-1-58430-279-7
[1. Chess—Fiction. 2. Behavior—Fiction. 3. Family problems—Fiction. 4. Schools—Fiction. 5. Inner cities—Fiction.]
I. Watson, Jesse Joshua, ill. II. Title.
PZ7.N4377478Che 2007
Fic]—dc22   2007010772

In my 'hood,
battles is fought every day.
Some on the street corner,
some in the park.
Warriors fall.
Kings is made.
Street gangs,
chess gangs.
Don't make
no difference.
It's all
a game
to me.

Opening Move

My Daddy
used to play chess
to calm his nerves
after workin' all day
in a room
with no windows.
I wanted to play him,
but he always say
I wasn't ready.
"This a man's game," he say.
"You a man?"

He made me play checkers
with my sister.
We watched him
from 'cross the room
just sittin' there,
movin' pieces

back
an' forth,
playin'
by hisself,
just starin'
at the board.
He pretended
to be both sides,
talkin' late into the night,
like he at war with
a ghost who wasn't there.

But sometimes the haze lifted,
and he noticed
we was in the room too.
When he put us to bed,
he told us stories
'bout all them crazy things
he done when he was young.
Them times I remember the best—
me, my sis, the twins, an' Mama,
all sittin' in bed
tellin' stories, laughin' an' screamin'
till it was time to go to sleep.
But that all stopped,
when my sister
died.
After that,
Daddy didn't tell stories no more.
Just sat by hisself
at that dang chessboard
till all the ghosts in his head
chased him
away
forever.

He never did show me
how to play.

Weeks an' months pass you by.
You don't notice till
you open your eyes one day
and it's a whole year later,
like God came down
and just took it away
without tellin' you.
Now I wake up
and I'm not sure
what day it is no more.
I get headaches
and lotsa things
make me mad—
like
my little brothers,
the twins.
They always gettin' me
in trouble,
findin' ways to make me crazy.

"Mommy!
Marcus ripped up my
homework!"
"Mommy!
Marcus poured grape drink
on the couch!"
Them weasels blame me
for everything,
and Mama believe 'em!
She make *me*
apologize
and clean up.
After that,
I just wanna
hurt somebody.
"You squeal on me again,
and there'll only
be one a you left."
POW!

Mama
always on the twins' side,
sayin' I'm almost
a teenager
and that I'm way
too big
to hit my little brothers.
"Even though you just eleven,
you almost as big as
your daddy now.
You need to set
an example
for the twins,
not send 'em
to the hospital," she say,
lightin' up her cigarette.
"They don't know better.
You should."
"They almost eight," I say.
"They ain't
so innocent."

I try
bein' a good brother.
I try
playin' with them
an' readin' with them
an' pretendin'
to be a space alien
so they can use
their secret weapons
on me.
But all they do is
try to see
who can make Marcus
go crazy first.

Like once,
they put my goldfish
in the toilet
and waited for me
to show up
before they flushed it
away.
That made me sad.
But then I got real angry
'cause that goldfish
was my friend.
The twins
just thought it was funny.
So I made 'em cry for what
they done.
Maybe next time,
they'll think twice
'bout messin' with me.

I got enough problems at home.
But school even worse.
Everyone out for me,
'specially Ms. Tate, the principal.
She always got her eye on me.
But worse
is havin' to see Latrell Jones
every day.
That fool
with his big mouth an' pretty-boy looks
is always up in my grill
'bout somethin'.
We used to be friends,
back when we was kids
and his mouth
wasn't so big.
We'd spend all afternoon
flippin'
on them old mattresses
in the lot 'cross the street.
But one day
Latrell smacked my sister
square in the face
just 'cause she laughed at him.

Me an' him got to havin' words,
and I told him to stay away
from my sister
or I'd pound him for real.
I became
his new number one
enemy
after that,
and he been after me
ever since.

As I growed up,
I got big real fast.
But in that head a Latrell's,
I just got fat.
Now he call me
Fat Albert,
thinkin' that's the worst
he can do to me.

Like today,
Latrell call me Fattie
in fronta some girls,
just to mess with
my head.
I tell him
I'm all muscle,
and I hit him
hard
in the arm so he know it.
But the more I hit,
the meaner he get.
He say
no one will ever
kiss me
and that I'll die
like them winos
in the park—
all lonely an' fat.

So I push him
and he push me.
Next thing I know,
I'm hittin' him in the face
till somebody
drag me offa him.

It's Ms. Tate.
I can smell her perfume
when she push me
into her office,
her big hands
on my sweaty shoulders.
I can hear Latrell
swearin'
he gonna get me back,
as the nurse clean up
that ugly mug a his.

Ms. Tate
say I'm trouble.
But I ain't got no time
for what she talkin' 'bout—
That hittin'
ain't the answer.
That I react
instead of think.
"This is your third fight
this month.
Do you want
to get kicked out of school?"
I know she won't do it,
on account a
she feel sorry for me
since my sister passed.
She think
I'm actin' out
'causa my pain.

"I don't care," I say
and put on my headphones.
Ms. Tate
throw up her hands
and just stare at me.
When I wear headphones,
I don't gotta talk
'bout things
like my sister
dyin'.

Ms. Tate say
I gotta get it
together.
"Maybe you can use
that anger
to break down barriers
instead of
creating new ones."
I wanna say
I'm not a angry guy,
that I'm not the one
she gotta worry 'bout.
But I can see
in the way she look at me
that she don't believe
I will turn it around.
So when she ask me
what I wanna be
when I grow up,
I say, "I wanna be
a boxer."
"Why is that, Marcus?"
"'Cause they pay you
to hit people."
She get this look
on her face,

like she don't approve.
I tell her,
"Fighters make more money
in one fight
than you'll ever make."
That one
get me a extra hour
of detention.

The next day,
when I see Ms. Tate,
she pointin' to her eyes,
like she sayin',
"I'm watching you."
I just shake my head.
What I ever do to her?
I think she prejudice
against big kids.
I think
if she keep lookin' at me
that way,
I might do something
that'll really
land me
in a heap
a trouble.

Later that week
Latrell try to corner me
in the boys' bathroom,
but I get him
in a headlock
and try to stick
that pretty-boy face a his
in the toilet.
When Ms. Tate show up,
she separate us and
tell Latrell to go to her office.
But me,
she got different plans for me.
"I've had it," she say,
holdin' up her big ol' hands.
"We'll try something new."
This time
she send me
to a room
I ain't been in for a long time—
the library.

When I get there,
I think
this the wrong place
'cause it be fulla kids
playin' chess,
like a bunch a know-it-alls.
This can't be for me,
unless Ms. Tate
done lost her marbles.
So I figure
I'll just disappear for a bit
and listen to my tunes.
But when I turn to leave,
some big dude
block my way.

He look like a fighter,
with a shaved head
an' eyes
that grab you.
"You think you can beat me?"
he ask.
I look 'round like
Who me?
He point
at a empty chessboard.
Everybody stop
and stare.
What else am I gonna say?
"Yeah, I can beat you."
He smile.
"Then come on,"
he say. "Beat me."

"So, what's your
opening move?" he ask.
I just sit there,
starin'
at the board.
I see the other kids
watchin' me,
laughin'
behind my back
'cause I don't know what to do.
So I say,
"This here my openin' move!"
and throw the board
on the floor.

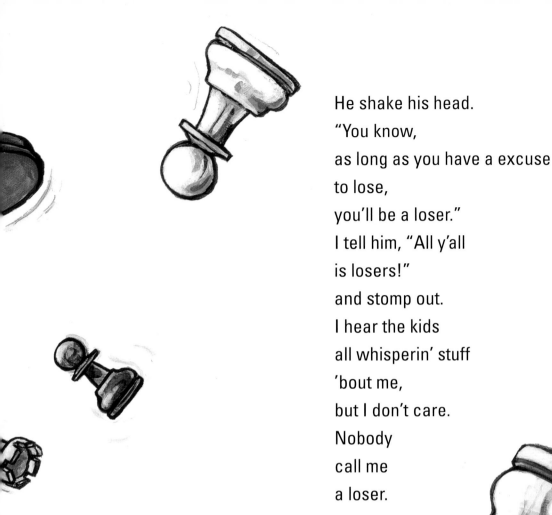

He shake his head.
"You know,
as long as you have a excuse
to lose,
you'll be a loser."
I tell him, "All y'all
is losers!"
and stomp out.
I hear the kids
all whisperin' stuff
'bout me,
but I don't care.
Nobody
call me
a loser.

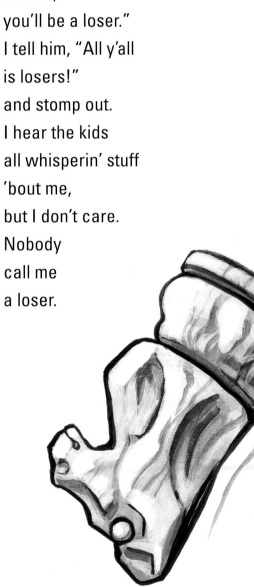

Whenever Mama's home,
I see her
smokin' her cigarettes
an' watchin' me
outta the corner a her eye,
just waitin'
for me to mess up.
She got two jobs now
and since Daddy left us,
her eyes
is always red
an' tired out.
She on edge a lot,
and she get on my case,
'bout how bad
I am at school,
'bout how I always
cause trouble,
and that all I ever do
is sit around,
playin' video games,
watchin' TV,
an' eatin' up all the food.

She always
yellin' at me,
askin' me to do stuff.
I watch the twins all the time.
Ain't that enough?
She say
I don't respect her.
Maybe that's true.
She can't get
no real job.
She can't hold on
to a husband.
And she can't keep
her kids alive
or outta trouble.

The only reason
I stay is 'cause
I got nowhere else
to go.

Mama say
that if I want to stay in this
house,
I gotta go see
a doctor
'bout my anger.
"Why you so angry
all the time?
Is it 'causa
your sister?
Is it 'causa
your daddy?"

Mama look at me,
waitin' for me
to bust out cryin'
or somethin'.
Instead, I yell,
"It's 'cause all y'all blame me
for everythin'!
It don't take no doctor
to tell me that!"
Mama tell me my anger
ain't normal,
that my anger
dangerous.
She act like I'm some
gangbangin' fool
ready to take out
the whole neighborhood.

If I keep gettin' into fights,
she say,
they gonna arrest me.
Or even worse,
she'll have to
send me *away*!
"IT AIN'T MY FAULT!" I yell
in her face.
Then she get this look
in her eyes,
like a scared little kid
and suddenly
I feel sick
to my stomach
'cause she lookin' at my
fist—
raised up
like I'm gonna hit her.

She glare at me.
"Shame on you," she cry,
shakin' her head.
Then Mama lock herself
in her room.
At that moment,
I hate myself
so much
I take my fist
and just hit it
against the wall,
over an' over.
I see the twins
down the hall.
They starin'
wide-eyed
at their crazy brother.
"What you lookin' at?!" I yell.
And they disappear
'round the corner.

I take a deep breath
and sit down
right where Mama
slammed the door on me.
I don't hear a peep
from inside her room.
So I wait
an' wait
an' wait.
When she finally come out,
she look at me
differently.
She don't say a word.
And my brothers
shut up too.
I know they afraid
a me.

Mama call my daddy,
who we ain't even seen
in six months.
She cryin' 'bout how she can't
get through to me and all.
I get on the phone.
Daddy tell me,
in that deep voice a his,
that I gotta be the man
a the house,
now that he ain't 'round
no more.

He say
not to hit my brothers
and don't never
ever hit Mama.
"One day
you'll go too far
and that
will be that.
You're the man now.
You got a obligation
to the family, Marcus."
"What 'bout you?" I say.
"Where your obligation at?"
That shut him up.

Middlegame

My friends is
Andre, Johnny, Floyd,
an' Double Z.
Mama don't like my friends.
But they a'ight.
They like me how I am.
They call me Hulk
and when we walk down the
street,
don't nobody mess with us.

My friends
is all good at somethin'.
For Double Z,
it's b-ball.
He NBA
all the way,
a real baller.
Me, I can't
shoot so good.
But Double Z don't mind.
Just give him the ball
and get outta the way.
He got mad skills, fer sure.

Sometimes
we go shopliftin'
at the market,
takin' little things
like candy an' Cokes.
Andre's the man in there.
He like to go
for the glory
and grab a steak or a chicken
or somethin' for his mama.
Me, I stick with the small things.
I ain't greedy.

Sometimes
we go with Floyd,
searchin' for a new wall
to tag.
Some a his art is real tight.
I wish
I could draw,
but I can't.
So I just act as the lookout.
I know the alleys
and shortcuts pretty good,
so we always got a way
to escape.

I may be big
but I can still run,
sometimes faster than
Floyd,
who always tryin'
to keep his spray cans
from fallin'
outta his
arms.

But Johnny's
the shorty with the rep.
He good with money,
always seem to get
what he want.
He like a businessman,
talkin' all the time and
hookin' us up with what we
need.
iPod? I get you a deal.
New Jordans? What color?
He say one day
he gonna be like
the 99 Cent Store a the
streets.
Best deals in town!

One day,
me an' my friends
is shootin' some hoops
over in the park.
I'm tryin'
to make some moves
to impress—
here come my
zigzaggin',
double-pumpin',
fade away three pointer
SMACKDOWN!
My boy Double Z
jump outta nowhere
and *slam* my highlight reel
out into the grass.
Man!
They make me
go chase the ball,
where it roll right up to,
guess who—

the chess dude.
He playin' chess
in the park,
where a bunch a guys
always pass the day,
and he right in the middle
a the action,
rippin'
through a game,
hittin'
the timer
an' bustin'
a move
every couple seconds.
Back
an' forth.
Bam! Move. *Bam!* Move.
Everybody 'round him
playin'
an' talkin'
trash.
"You mine today."
"Is that all you got?"
"Your queen is my lady now!"
"Somebody arrest this fool
for loiterin' on my game!"

Only this dude,
he play it real cool,
don't talk
like the rest of 'em.
Everybody callin' him CM,
and treatin' him
like he somethin'
special.

I grab the ball,
but before I take off
I see him beat a guy
in like ten seconds flat.
And all he say is,
"Checkmate. Next."

CM see me
and nod.
"Control,
that's the name
of the game," he say.
"That's what chess
can teach you."
I give him a look. *So?*

He look over at my boyz on
the court
who is hootin' an' hollerin'
for the ball an' still bustin' up
'bout my bein' posterized
by Double Z.
"Looks like you can use
some of that control," CM say.
I shake my head.
"Hey, I got game, ol' man."
The other chess guys go,
"Oooh!"
like it's some kinda throwdown,
but CM just raise his eyebrow.
"Is that what you call that?
Game?
That must be why the ball
is all the way over here
instead of on the court
where it belong."

His guys pop a gut laughin'.
I palm the ball. "I don't see you
playin' for the Knicks," I say.
CM laugh. "I only play with winners."
He set up his game again.
"See, you think you're a king,
but you're just a pawn.
You're not playing to your
strengths.
You got brains somewhere
in that head a yours.
You just gotta use 'em."
I stare him down good,
but I can't think a nothin'
to say back at him.
He look at me
for a long time,
like he tryin'
to read my mind.
"You gonna hurt somebody, son?"
"Who say I'm gonna
hurt somebody?"

"You did, son.
Got your fist
wound up in a ball,
all ready to get Ali on me."
I give him The Face.
"You crazy."
"Used to be," he say.

Then he get up. "Gimme
the ball."
He grab it outta my hands,
then before I can stop him
he boot it back to the court.
"Hey! What'ya doin'?!"
"Come with me," he say,
then start walkin' down
the line a chess tables.
I look back at the court.
They already playin'
without me.
"Come on, little big man.
We got a different game
going on over here."

CM walk over
to a chessboard behind a tree
where some kid
is sittin' by hisself.
I know this dude
from around.
He my age.
His name is Kevin,
but we call him Li'l K.
Why he playin' chess?

Li'l K look up at me.
"You wanna play?"
Him I know I can beat,
even if I don't know nothin'.
But then I think a my daddy and
how the only people
I seen play this game so far
was crazy.
I look back to the court,
but CM say, "Come on little big man,
take a load off."
He hold out a chair for me.
"Kevin ain't gonna bite,"
he say, smilin'.
I sit. "Let's make this quick."

Then I see
that all my pieces
is white.
"Why I gotta be white?"
I say.
"White always gets to go
first," CM say.
"You got that right,"
I say back.
He laugh. "You know how
to play?"
Ain't no one 'round
to laugh at me this time.
But I act all cool.
"Maybe. But let me see
how you play first."

Li'l K smile. "See,
that's your side of the board," he say,
pointin' to my white pieces.
"Anything you do on your side
is up to *you*.
Anytime
you in a bad spot,
it's 'cause *you*
got yourself there."
I shake my head
"Man, you sound
just like Ms. Tate."
CM chime in,
"She's looking out for you, you know?"
"Nah. She out to get me," I say.
"I ain't done nothin' to her,
but she think I'm the bad guy."
CM smirk.
"Oh, it's like *that*, huh?
You play that game,
you gonna get beat
every time."

"What game is that?" I ask.
"The blame game.
You know—
If it hadn't been
for my mama—
If my teacher
had just minded her own
business—
If the police
hadn't been cruisin' by
that night—"

I cut him off.
"Are we gonna play
or what?"

Li'l K show me
how the game go.
Chess is like
two armies goin' at it.
The object
is to get the king.
"But if you
don't have a plan," Li'l K say,
"you gonna lose."

He show me
how each piece move.
Like the castle
goes straight an' sideways,
an' the bishop
crosses over,
an' the horse
does a L-shape thing.
I like the queen,
'cause she do
whatever she want.

He show me
how to capture the enemy
and get to the
king.
I say, "Okay, okay. I got it. Let's go!"
I know the strongest one
gonna win.
So I'll just hit him
with everythin' I got
so I can take this fool.
I jump in,
charging' ahead.
I'm gonna get that king!
Six moves later,
Li'l K say,
"Checkmate."

Say what?
"That means I beat you."
He grinnin' ear to ear.
I growl, "Yeah, yeah. Let's
go again.
You just caught me off guard,
that's all."
We go again,
me bangin' ahead
with my front line a pawns,
lookin' to do some damage.
I'm playin' my game,
weavin' in an' out,
zigzaggin'—
but that only get me ten moves.
"Checkmate," he say again.

I'm seein' green. I can feel the Hulk
comin' out—
CM put his hands on my shoulders.
"You gotta slow down,
little big man.
Think ahead
three moves," CM say.
"If you can't see
what's gonna happen next,
you're dead."

We go again,
but Li'l K keep movin'
too fast
and I can't keep up.
CM coachin' me
from the sidelines.
"Think about
your middlegame.
Don't just go
for the glory.
Think about
where
you wanna be next.

If you're lookin'
too far down the road,
you'll miss his attack."
But Li'l K cuttin' me off
with every move,
beatin' me left
an' right.
I can't see
where I wanna go,
'cause he always there.
Dang!
How'd he get so *good*?!

Finally
I can't stand
this dumb game
no more.
I get up to leave.
CM say, "You know,
the best players
come up from the streets.
That's
where the struggle is."
"Whatever," I say, holdin' up
my hands.

"Check this out." CM sit down
in my place
and move the game back
three moves.
He put his finger
on my queen.
"It's simple, really.
If you touch a piece
and you don't know
where you're goin',
that's a bad move.
It's all about
the next three moves.
You gotta outthink
your opponent.
If you know
where he's going,
then you can beat him
by blockin' his moves
or doin'
the unexpected."

He see me lookin' over at my
friends,
who is mixin' it up
on the court
with a bunch a gangbangers
who hang 'round here.
"Is it worth spendin'
the rest of your life
in prison
all because
you didn't think
about what
was gonna happen
next?"
For the first time
I notice the tattoos
on his neck.

"You was sent up?" I ask.
"For real?"
He frown.
"Yeah.
That's where I learned
to play chess."
I just shake my head.
"A con man.
Figures."

CM don't say nothin',
just make
a different move
than I did,
and in three steps
he beat Li'l K,
who ain't too happy 'bout it.
"I still won, right?" Li'l K ask.

My boyz is callin' me
back to the court.
"I gotta go," I say.
CM say calmly,
"Three moves
is all it takes
to change the outcome
of the game."
I head to the court
and don't look back.
My head hurt
from thinkin' too much.

That night I'm walkin' home
and it's dark out.
None a the streetlights
is workin', as usual.
It get dark early now,
but Mama don't say nothin'
as long as I get home
for dinner.
And right when I'm thinkin'
'bout chowin' down
on some a her beef stew,
that's when I hear
Latrell.

"Hey, hey, hey. It's Fat Albert!"
But his voice
ain't jokin' around
this time.
I could keep walkin' but—
he shout, "You want some more
a me, Fattie?"
I can feel my blood
boiling.
"Ain't it past your bedtime?"
I say.
He step out
onto the sidewalk,
and even though it's dark
I can still see
he got a coupla tough shorties
with him.

But I don't walk away.
I just say,
"Oh, so you need your
friends
to take the Hulk down."
They take a step closer.
Latrell grinnin'.
"You ain't no Hulk.
You just a fat boy
who sister did all the talkin'
for him."
That's when I snap.
I rush 'em,
snarlin' an' growlin'.
The Hulk will pound you!
BAM! POW!

But this ain't like the comix.
And they right,
I ain't no real Hulk.
After my first charge
they jump me
and start kickin'
an' hittin'
till I can't hardly move
no more.

"Look at him," Latrell say,
laughin'.
"You ain't so tough now, Fattie."
They all spit on me
and leave me layin' there
alone,
in the dark.
Finally
I get up,
bruised an' beat.
It take me a hour
to drag myself home.

When I open the door
to our apartment,
Mama start yellin' at me
for bein' so late—
but when she see
what they done to me,
she don't say a word,
just hold me
in her arms
like she used to
when I was little
and the only one
that mattered.

I tell her I'm sorry
for wantin' to hit her
and that I don't wanna
hit nobody
no more.
She say it's gonna be okay.
"We just need some love,
right baby?"
I don't say a thing,
but I know she right.

The next morning,
even the twins is nice to me.
They let me watch
my TV show
without a fight.
They just sit there
real quiet,
no name callin'
or tryin'
to get me in trouble.
"Did you hit 'em back?"
was all they asked,
but I didn't say nothin'.

Then Mama come in,
tellin' us
to get dressed.
"We gonna go visit
your sister," she say.
I don't wanna go
to no cemetery.
My body
ache too much.
My head hurt
and I ain't in a good mood.
But Mama
just take my hand
and we go.

On the bus
I sit next to Mama.
It's been over a year,
but I can still remember
my sister
the way she used to be.
She giggled
like a little girl,
even though she was big
like me.

We liked to hide
in the closet
and eat
all the ice cream.
She told me
alla her secrets
and I told her
alla mine.
She was the one
I trusted the most
and we talked 'bout
all the crazy things
we was gonna do
together.

But
then she got real sick
and started blackin' out
from time to time.
They say
she had a "cardiac sickness,"
but she refused
to sit still and rest
like the doctors wanted.
Then one day
we was runnin' around
playin' tag,
and laughin' so hard,
all outta breath.

All of a sudden
she stopped
and got this strange look
on her face.
Her eyes got real distant,
like she didn't see me no more.
She fell down
and I thought
she just fainted again.
I waited
for her to wake up.
But she never did.

They say
it was all 'cause
the walls
in her heart
was too thick
and that's why
she had herself
a heart attack.
I used to think
only ol' people
had heart attacks,
but I guess anyone
can die
when your time
is up.

We standin' by her grave,
and while Mama clean off the
leaves,
I can see she cryin'.
She tryin'
to keep it all inside
so we don't notice.
My little brothers
is standin' next to me,
lookin' at the tombstone,
when one of 'em say
"I miss my sister."
I ask what he miss
'bout her
and he say
when she was here,
I never hit 'em.
"Yeah," I say.
"When she was 'round,
we never did fight."

After she left us,
that's when things started
fallin' apart,
an' everyone
got so angry,
an' Daddy left
an' then there was no one
to listen to me
no more.
Now I wish
I could see my sister
alive an' smilin' at me,
not just her name
on some grave
in a stupid cemetery.

Endgame

The next day at school
I stay away
from Double Z an' them.
They won't understand
why we don't go stomp
on Latrell an' his boyz.
Instead,
I look for CM.
He in the old library,
cleanin' up.
He look at my busted lip
an' swollen eye
and don't ask how
or why.
He just nod his head.
"I was hopin'
you would come," he say.
I stand there for a minute.
Then I ask,
"You wanna play?"
He shrug.
"Well, you got your opening.
You're here."

He lay out the chessboard.
"So, you wanna run
through this obstacle course
I'm gonna put out for you?
Or you wanna
control the offense?"
"Control," I say.
"Yeah, I figured you'd say that.
How you gonna do it?"
"By thinkin' ahead
three steps," I say.
He nod again.
"Once you got your
middlegame,
then your endgame
becomes clear."

"Where you wanna
end up?" CM ask.
I don't say nothin'.
He wait,
then say,
"You'll figure it out."

We play
and he beat me.
But this time
I last fifteen moves.
"That's progress," he say.
He set up the board
for another round,
but as I'm watchin' him,
this question pop into
my head and outta my mouth.
"You was a troublemaker
when you was my age,
wasn't you?"
He stop and get this look
in his eye.
"Yep. Always looking
for trouble."
"And what happened?" I ask.
"Trouble found me," he say.

Over the next month
CM an' me play every day
after school.
We even talk
'bout stuff that's botherin' me,
like Latrell
an' my sister,
an' Daddy
not bein' 'round
no more.
He show me that
all them chess pieces
is like a family.
That when one fall,
the others carry on.
They have to.
But when one win,
the whole family
win.

Then one afternoon
CM look at his watch,
and sit there
like he waitin'
for somethin'
to happen.
"What?" I say. "It's your move."
"Nah." He smile. "It's yours."
And that's when
the door open
and Latrell
walk in.

I stare at him hard.
He freeze when he see me.
I jump to my feet,
waitin' for CM
to stop me.
But CM just sit there,
starin' at the board,
a little smirk
on his face.
I look at my fists,
all balled up
and ready to do
some hurtin'.

Latrell look like
he don't know
what to do.
But with CM right next to me,
I can't help but think
'bout my next
three moves
and what
could happen here.
I could beat Latrell
to a pulp,
somethin' he deserve
for real.
But then
maybe Ms. Tate   *Know*
would really   *my opponent.*
kick me outta school.   *Know*
Maybe even   *his next move.*
have me arrested.   *Do*
Then what?   *the unexpected.*
I remember   I glare
what CM told me   at Latrell,
'bout my game plan.   then suddenly
                               the words
                               just come outta
                               my mouth.

"You think you can beat me?"
I say.
His face
scrunch up,
all confused.
He shoot a look
over at CM,
who nod
and offer Latrell
his chair at the chessboard.
"You ain't afraid a me,
is ya?" I ask.
Latrell
get all huffy.
"I can beat you, Fat Albert."
I look him straight
in the eye.
"Well, come on then.
Beat me."

I can see he know
'bout as much
as I did
when I played Li'l K.
But that don't stop him
from gettin' all up in my face.

"I'm gonna take you down," he say.
I try the CM attitude,
no trash talkin',
no reactin'.
Only action.
I wanna win.
Latrell stomp ahead
with his pawns.
I ignore his charge
and focus on that king.
I know what he gonna do
even before he do it.
After 'bout twenty moves
I see my openin'.
There it is,
the king
with no way out.

"Checkmate," I say,
just like CM.
Latrell stare at the board.
He angry.
"You just got lucky, Fattie!
Let's go again," he say.

I beat Latrell
three more times.
I actually start to feel bad
for him.
He just like I was,
all talk an' no brains.
So I make him a deal—
he don't call me
Fat Albert no more
and me an' CM
will teach him
a thing or two 'bout chess.
Then maybe
he stand a chance.
Latrell stare at the board
for a long time.
Then he say
"Okay."

After a hour
of lessons from CM,
I can see
Latrell startin'
to get it.

"How 'bout a rematch
tomorrow?" I ask him.
He look at CM.
"Maybe."
CM tell him
to take a board home
and practice.
Latrell seem unsure,
but CM put one a the extra boards
in his hands.
When Latrell get up
to leave,
he stop
and look at his feet.
Then he say somethin'
so quiet
I can barely hear him.
He whisper,
"Sorry
'bout your sister,
Marcus."

I don't say nothin',
just nod.
He look at me
outta the corner
a his eye,
nod back,
and head on his way.

Then it's just me an' CM
alone
in the library again.
I start settin' up
the board.
"You wanna play me?" I ask.
He smile. "Sure.
You got CM potential."
I laugh. "Say, why they call
you that anyway?" I ask.
"Well, I'm not playin'
in the competitions,
so I can't really be a Grand Master,
or what they call a GM.
I'm not that good.
But folks in my neighborhood
call me CM,
'cause to them I'm the Chess Man.
That's all they ever see me doin',
you know?
Then in the park,
they started callin' me Check Mate
'cause that's all I ever say.
Checkmate.

But now the kids here call me
Chess Master.
And that sounds about right.
Bein' here,
I feel like
I've figured out
my endgame.
Just like you're doin'."

CM tell me
he startin' a new program
for school.
A chess gang, he call it.
"We gonna rumble
every Friday night,
like warriors.
Play through to the morning.
That's how you
really earn
your badge of honor."
Warriors.
I like that.
I think 'bout my friends.
They all good at somethin'.
Why can't I be good at this?
"Maybe I can be in it," I say.
"Maybe," CM say. "Think you're
good enough?"

"Hey, I can hold my own
against a Chess Master."
He smile, noddin' his head.
"Hey, what about Latrell?"
I ask.
He raise a eyebrow.
"I mean, we gotta have
somebody to teach, right?"
I say.
"'Cause trouble
just gonna keep findin' him."
CM bust out laughin'.
"Yeah, I think you're
figurin' out your endgame."

I finish settin' up the board.
"Ready?" I ask.
"Bring it on," CM say.
And we start playin',
just two warriors
in the library
doin' their thing.